A
MW01089539
BULLIES
DON'T
SCARE ME!
ILLUSTRATED BY
FELICIA WHALEY

Bullies Don't scare me!

Published by Andre' Renee Writes Publishing Company

ISBN 13: 978-1979771726

ISBN 10: 1979771723

Printed in the U.S.A.

www.arwrites.com

Bullies Don't scare me!

Andre' Renee Harris

Illustrated by

Felicia Whaley

Preface

This book provides an opportunity for families to spend time together while enjoying exceptional literature.

Eric is a nice and playful seven-year-old boy,

who is very tall for his age.

He was adopted when he was a baby by his mothers, Jean and Peggy.

Every day after school, both of his moms would pick him up in front of the school.

The other children would meet their parents there too.

This is a new school for Eric, so his moms usually take him for ice cream after they pick him up. This is when they ask him how his day went.

One day Eric was quiet, and he didn't want to eat his ice cream. His moms were puzzled, “This is your favorite,” they both said.

Jean asked Eric, "What's wrong, baby?" Eric replied in a frightened voice, “Nothing, but this is a mean school.”

Peggy asked, "Are your classmates mean because of how tall you are?" Eric said, "Yes," but his parents weren't convinced that was true.

A week later as they were going for ice cream, one of his mothers asked "How was school?" This time, Eric had tears in his eyes, and asked,

"Can we move?"

Both moms were concerned, so the following day, they went to his school and asked his teachers about the situation.

Due

The teacher replied, “He may be bullied because he has two moms.” They agree to see if the children can work it out amongst each other.

Later that day, his parents explained why he need not be afraid of bullies, and to always show people love and respect no matter how mean they are.

Sometimes bullies are mean because they are scared themselves and quick to follow the leader of the loudest person in the crowd.

Eric said, "Moms, I know I don't know my dad, but I'm in a very loving family. I also know that not all families look the same. I believe the mean kids need to know that your parents are those who love you always."

Both parents are proud of him.

The next day, Eric confronted the kids who were bullying him.

He said, "I will treat you with respect because this is what my mothers taught me; no matter how mean you act.”

All the children in the class heard what was said, and they smiled. They all began to say nice comments towards one another. Eric spoke with confidence, “Bullies don't scare me anymore!” The rest of the children repeated it too.

“Bullies don't scare me.”

Andre' Renee Harris

As a writer of children's books, I believe teaching children early to get along with one another is paramount to life, peace and growth. In my series of children's books, the goal is to do just that. Our future generation is the most important focus of my life. My purpose is to channel all the positive energy I can into my writing. I strongly believe that children are never too young to be exposed to a variety of cultures. Humanity will depend on us. As caretakers of young minds, we must do our due diligence when educating them. We are tasked with cultivating a new generation, so that they will be afforded social provisions to take humanity to greater heights.

Education is the fertile ground needed to plant our children. Nurturing children through literature brings wonder and amazement to their lives. As they grow, it becomes more apparent how vital it is to forge strong alliances, among all people, across all nations and beliefs.

Made in the USA
Middletown, DE
28 October 2021